MW00893269

This book belongs to:

____

If found, please contact:

____

____

Made in the USA
Monee, IL
24 June 2021

72176286R10061